Cosy Burrow Books

VALKYRIE ACADEMY DRAGON ALLIANCE
Book Seven

WARNED

I0593075

"You might think you know the stories of the Valkyrie, Loki, and Odin, but you only know the tip of the iceberg. If these are a few of your favorite characters, you are in for a treat. Set in the backdrop of Asgard, the wingless Valkyries are on a quest to prove themselves and protect their dragons. This high-flying adventure will leave the reader wanting more." Neila F., Line Editor, Red Adept Editing

Valkyrie Academy Dragon Alliance Books

Cosy Burrow Books

VALKYRIE ACADEMY DRAGON ALLIANCE

WARNED

KATRINA COPE

ISBN: 978-0-6486613-6-8

Michael ~ your support means the world to me

GET UPDATES & NOTIFICATIONS OF GIVEAWAYS

Would you like a FREE copy of Marked?
Visit here:
https://www.katrinacopebooks.com/valkyrie-academy-dragon-alliance

Through this link you can sign up for my newsletter and receive a FREE copy of Marked plus updates about my fantasy books, sales and notification of giveaways.

- CHAPTER ONE -

My heart thumps against my chest, an urgent beat with a touch of desperation, dying to be free. The need to close my eyes is strong, but I don't want to miss out on the thrill of what is happening. The wind catches my hood and blows it off, leaving my head bare and my ears exposed to its force. The gusts squeal against my ears, thrumming against my eardrums. Breaking through the final layer of cloud, we plummet headfirst toward the ground several thousand feet below. My nose is numb, and my cheeks are burning from the cold.

A cry of exhilaration erupts from behind me, and I turn my head away from the progressing view to find Hildr hooking her legs around Drogon's neck. Hildr flings her arms up in the air as they also nosedive toward the ground. Wearing an invigorated smile, Eir dives not far behind her. Naga's plummet isn't as direct as Drogon's and is slightly angled for a slower descent.

A few seconds behind is a red streak. Tanda is descending with us but at a slower pace. Britta sits at the base of Tanda's neck. Her face is white, and her eyes hold a strange mixture of excitement and terror.

I smirk. It is Britta's first flight on a dragon, and I'm sure she's stressing right now. Tanda decided to join us after the fight with the dark elves. It was a strange sight to see, a welcome sight—the red eyes of the dragon burning with friendship instead of hate and anger. I only hope that Tanda's mother will approve. Perhaps if Ness sees that Tanda has settled in well and we are taking care of her, she will not be so reluctant to follow Eingana's rules and give up one of her hatchlings every time she has a clutch. Hopefully, Ness will see that handing over her eggs to the Valkyries to honor the alliance is not all doom and gloom when they bond with a wingless Valkyrie. And possibly, we can work together to make a better alliance.

I face the front again and see that the ground is only a few hundred feet away. It is hard, but I have to place my full trust in Elan. She is an experienced flyer, and I'm sure she won't crash into the ground. Still, the sudden descent gets my heart pumping and the adrenaline rushing through my blood. I shove the black strands of hair out of my face and fling them behind me. I can feel the wind whipping at them. The ground lunges up at us until the last second when Elan tilts slightly with her wings spread and flicks her tail. We change direction and glide along the top of Asgard's surface before ascending again into the sky. My heartbeat slows, almost thanking me for the change of direction as it settles down.

So what do you think about that? Elan's voice pierces through my thoughts. *Would you like to do it again?*

I puff out a large stream of air. "I think I'm good, Elan."

Does that mean you want to do it again? She asks as she swivels her head around and smirks over her shoulder.

"No, Elan. I think my heart's had enough excitement for today."

It's nice to spend time like this with Elan. We haven't had much time lately. There has been so much going on, but I know the other riders must bond with their dragons more, especially Britta and Tanda, seeing as they are newly coupled. Elan, being the dragon leader's daughter, knows this is important in trying to build the bond between dragons and the wingless Valkyries.

As we fly over the plain, the other three dragons line up beside us. They all beat their wings in time, staying on the same level. My ears are burning with cold from the recent descent, and I grab for the hood of my dragon-scale cloak and pull it over my head.

Elan peers over her shoulder. *Are you feeling warm?*

I can feel her toasty scales underneath my legs, and they are slowly heating me, spreading the cozy temperature through the rest of my body. The dragon-scale cape is also blocking out most of the cold air. "Almost." I tug at the edges of my hood and grip the front of my cloak closed, leaving my face only barely exposed from underneath the hood.

You two dragons stay here for a moment or hover behind us at a distance. Elan telepathically speaks with me and the other dragons, addressing us all at once. *I just want to do something first.*

Drogon nods once, and Elan flaps her wings, increasing her speed. At first, I wonder what she's doing, but I trust her, and I push any concern out of my head, enjoying the ride. As she flaps her wings some more, two white dots appear on the horizon on either side of her head. My eyes fix on them, and I continue to watch them as we approach. After we devour the space between us, I realize that they are the white wings of the winged Valkyries from the academy. They are probably the guards doing their rounds and checking on everything. Elan progresses toward them at a rapid rate.

"What are you doing, Elan?" I ask.

Not much. I'm just checking on the Valkyries.

She flaps her wings harder, and the gap between the Valkyries and us decreases. Her scales disappear from underneath me until I feel like I'm flying on air, with nothing holding me up. Before I know it, Elan is flying between the two Valkyries. She slows down and travels next to them for a stretch, and we sit in silence, listening to their conversation.

I know with my cape on and Elan being invisible, I am also invisible except for my face. But if I keep it hidden under my cloak, they will not be able to see me. Even Elan's saddle straps are invisible when she is. It was only the other day that I sewed scales on them for moments like this.

"Did you see that warrior in the halls of Valhalla last night? He is so handsome, and I swear he was checking me out."

The second Valkyrie giggles. "Those einherjar can be so flirtatious. But who can blame them? We are so gorgeous."

The first one slightly squeals when she chuckles. "Well, I don't mind having to wait on them if they treat us like that. It gets me all flittery inside."

As *we* fly next to them, I wonder what they are talking about. I know the einherjar are the warriors that they reap in preparation for Ragnarok, but it's the way they are talking about them that I don't understand. Then I remember how Harut makes me feel at times, and I feel my cheeks warming. My thoughts vanish when the Valkyrie on the right looks around then peers at the Valkyrie on the left.

"There's some kind of strange breeze in the air today. Can you feel it?" the first one asks the other.

"Yeah. I can feel some weird wind. It comes from that way." The left Valkyrie points in the direction of the one on the right.

The Valkyrie on the right frowns. "I thought it was coming from that way." She points in the direction of the left Valkyrie.

The left Valkyrie's forehead furrows. They fly some more and slowly close the gap between them as they talk. Elan rises slightly above them.

"Do you feel the breeze coming from above now?" the Valkyrie on the right asks.

"Yes. That's strange. Since when does the breeze blow downwards?"

I continue to rise and fall slightly with the beat of Elan's wings, and after a few more wingbeats, she suddenly she appears underneath me. She twists her head around and drops it, descending in front of the two Valkyries' faces as they fly toward her.

Boo! Elan says telepathically while showing off her vicious smile.

The two Valkyries' faces lose all color just before they dart to either side, separating themselves, then dive to the ground. Elan's laughter echoes through the valley, her head jerking up and down with the movement.

"Oh, Elan. That was nasty." I throw a hand over my smile.

My legs jerk sideways a few times as her chuckles rattle her torso. *Yeah, but fun. Besides, the winged Valkyries deserve it. They've been nothing but nasty to you and your friends and all the dragons.*

"Don't push it, though, Elan. I think we're starting to make some progress with some of them. You don't want to undo all the hard work we've been doing."

She shrugs. *They'll get over it. I have many years to catch up on, and that's just to pay them back for the way they have treated the dragons. It won't surprise me if the Valkyries are behind stealing the eggs.*

"What makes you think that, Elan?"

I can't imagine what the zmey creature would want with our eggs. It must be working for someone or some organization. Unless it is starving and only lives off dragon eggs.

At the mention of the zmey, my guilt slurs in a sludgy well within my stomach. I still haven't managed to speak to Loki. I saw him on that hill after the fight with the dark elves, but I couldn't get up to him before he disappeared. It is so frustrating. I am dying for some answers that I can't get from anyone but Loki. Not only that, I hear that it is Loki who turns into the zmey creature, the one that steals the eggs. Yet at the same time, he represents the dragons in front of Odin, making out like he's their friend. I need to know for sure if the zmey is him because I need to sort this out. I don't like keeping secrets from the dragons.

You're awfully quiet, Elan says.

"Hmm. I have a lot on my mind."

- CHAPTER TWO -

Elan lands at the site, and I climb off her back.

She nudges me with her shoulder. *Well, I hope you soon share with me what's on your mind. It's so boring when you're quiet like this.*

A deep twinge of guilt circulates through my torso. I'm still not sure what to do with the Loki and dragon debacle. At the same time, I don't want to hold anything back from Elan. It's tearing me up.

Three loud thumping sounds synchronize around us. Drogon, Naga, and Tanda have landed with their passengers on their backs.

Britta's face is ecstatic with excitement. "That was awesome!" She is almost yelling. "Never in my life did I think that would happen to me." She turns around and grins at Tanda with eyes full of adoration. The red dragon's eyes are wary, yet there is no harshness in them. The bond has not yet been established, although I can see improvement and all signs of encouragement that they will bond shortly. "Can I pet your nose?" Britta raises her hand toward Tanda but doesn't move forward.

For a moment, Tanda's eyes open wide and focus on Britta's hand without saying anything. After a while, she nods once.

Britta approaches slowly, not wanting to startle the dragon. Gradually, she runs her hand up the dragon's scaly nose. There are still some signs of the big gashes inflicted by the winged Valkyries the other day. But they have healed well with the help of Anita's ointments.

As Britta approaches, she says, "I'm so sorry that the winged Valkyries have maltreated you. I would never do that. Please believe me. Hopefully, something will be worked out between the dragons and the winged Valkyries to stop this barbarity."

I'm knocked aside, and I turn to see that Eir has lost her balance and landed on me. On her other side, I spot a large blue object. Naga has tilted his head and nudged Eir's side. His big eyes are staring at her affectionately.

She cackles. "Sorry, Kara. He's just so excitable."

I chuckle with her. Those two have completely bonded, and Naga is such a sweet dragon.

Elan interrupts our chuckle. *I have to be off.*

The smile disappears from my face. "That's sudden. Where are you going?"

I'm going to see Mother. Elan looks at Tanda. *I have to report back about Tanda's progression and the bonds between Drogon and Hildr, and Naga and Eir. I'm sure my mother would be very interested to know that certain young dragons have been happy to adjust and bond with the wingless Valkyries and that they share a kindness. Hopefully, this will give her insight on what to do about the whole alliance.*

"I hope she succeeds in negotiating something better," I say. "Although she may have a challenge because Odin and Mistress Sigrun don't have any faith in the wingless Valkyries."

She nods once. *We shall see. Drogon, Naga, and Tanda, you need to return to your stalls while I'm gone to make it appear that you are honoring the alliance. I don't want Odin to have any reason to make it worse.*

The three dragons nod their acknowledgment in unison.

Elan looks at each one of us in turn. *Bye for now.* She pushes off into the air, her golden scales disappearing under the sun.

Hildr climbs down from Drogon's back, clasping his horns as she slides to the side. Her feet hit the ground with a thud.

It reminds me of how awkward her ride would have been without something to grab on to. I look at my three friends. "I know what we need to do. We need to make some saddles."

Hildr scowls at me. "Why would I need a saddle?"

My jaw drops as I look at Hildr in disbelief. "You definitely need a saddle. I don't know how you hold on to Drogon with the way his wings are attached to his front legs."

Drogon huffs and shakes his horny head, looking displeased.

I hold up my hand in defense toward him. "It's nothing against you, Drogon. I like your unique build. It just means she's got less to hang on to without a saddle. She can't hook her legs behind your shoulder blades because your wings are in the road. Besides wrapping her legs around your neck, the only thing she can hold on to is your horns if she manages not to get jabbed in the face by all the other horns."

"I don't mind," Hildr says. "We just had an exhilarating flight with my legs wrapped around Drogon's neck and without a saddle."

"I know, Hildr. And you're very clever with that, but I prefer to know that you have a saddle because it's easier to hang on to, especially if we have to go into battle again and ride the dragons. The dragons may be too distracted to catch us or have less opportunity to drop everything to rescue us."

Hildr turns around and embraces Drogon's nose then touches her forehead to his snout before looking up. "All right. I guess we'll do it. I would rather partake in a fight. It's much more exciting than learning how to thread a needle through some leather."

"I certainly want to sit on a saddle," Britta says. "It's hard to hang on to Tanda's large camel lump in the middle of her back. Don't get me wrong—I love her unusual look. It's just harder to hook my legs around her neck. And I have to yank at her fur. It probably hurts, but she won't let me know."

Tanda's eyes dart to Britta, and she huffs slightly, releasing billows of smoke from her nostrils. Britta touches Tanda tenderly on the nose. At first, Tanda seems apprehensive, but she puts up with it.

Eir gives Naga one last cuddle. "See you soon, Naga. Hopefully, you will only be up in the stalls for a little while longer. In any case, I'll come and visit you soon to brighten it up for you." She runs her hand down the side of his face.

The three dragons push up in unison and flap their wings as they head toward the dragon stalls. It reminds me of how there are so many more dragons within the stalls. The majority of them are vicious and upset, especially with the Valkyries because of the way the winged ones have treated them. Many have been persecuted over the years by the winged Valkyries. The Valkyries claim that they need to practice fighting against those kinds of beasts.

When the dragons have disappeared, we go to the tanning yard and remove pieces of leather from soaking in the saline solution. Then we get to work.

Hildr groans. "I hate doing this. It's just so boring and mundane." The hide lies on a large, flat stone, and she rubs her sharp-edged rock over the coat, removing all the fur from the outside.

"I find it peaceful." Eir's face is relaxed as she works on her leather.

I brush aside the fur I have removed and study the smooth leather underneath. "I can't say that it's my favorite thing. Although I certainly appreciate the things I have made,

19

including the saddle for Elan and my cloak, so I'm going to keep making things."

Britta brushes her hand over the skin, works on removing the remaining fur, then cuts it into strips. She copies my movements as though they are instructions. We all work together on our different saddles, remaining at the same stage. A saddle is not something we make every day and is not something the winged Valkyries teach, as they rarely need to ride anything.

Britta releases a frustrated sigh, and I look at her.

"I can't believe how Mistress Sigrun treats you," she says. "I know she doesn't like wingless Valkyries, but you have defended all of the Valkyries with Eir and Hildr's help. And then to hear that Mistress Sigrun wiped her hands of you in front of the other senior Valkyries, acting like you're worthless even though you saved her and helped defend

Asgard and the Valkyries." She shakes her head in disgust.

"Yeah, I know. It stinks, but it's not a surprise. It doesn't seem to matter how well I do. She still turns around and slaps me across the face for my effort. Even after I protected her from the dark elves, she still made out like I was in the wrong."

A rock clatters around the corner, and the four of us pivot to stare at the spot. Beautiful white wings frame the thin, petite body and the beautiful face that studies us from only a short distance away.

"Rota?" The name tumbles out of my mouth, and my brow furrows.

She glances down at the ground briefly, fiddling with her fingers before looking at me. "What Mistress Sigrun did wasn't nice, but she's in a tough place. If she doesn't do everything that Odin and the senior Valkyries want, she'll be stripped of her title and possibly her wings. As you can imagine, it would be a very harsh treatment. If there's any threat against her, she is naturally going to rebuke everything that you've done and protect herself and her own interests." Her face takes on a vacant look. "If a Valkyrie loses her wings..." She pauses and looks at us, her face suddenly overcome with guilt. "Well, then she is defamed—stripped of everything she's worth. They may even kill the Valkyrie, and if they don't, the Valkyrie may end up killing herself."

"Welcome to our world." Hildr doesn't hide the sarcasm her voice. Her top lip lifts into a sneer as she stares at Rota.

Rota's shoulders slump. "I know. And I'm sorry. It's a hard path to follow either way. I was born into a prestigious title. I have much to lose if I associate with wingless Valkyries. I would have to deny it. I could lose a lot, like the position that I may be getting when I'm older. Not only that, Odin and the senior Valkyries would disgrace my family as well— my mother would be shamed."

Apprehensively, she steps closer to us and squats next to Hildr. "May I help? I like working with leather."

"Knock yourself out!" Without a moment's hesitation, Hildr pushes backward, sliding on her backside away from the leather.

Hildr watches Rota as she works nimbly, her fingers showing off her experience.

"Thank you for helping." I pull a strand of leather through a hole and pull tightly, securing the pieces together.

Rota's smile is sad. "Oh, no problem. Perhaps one day, I'll get to ride a dragon too."

"Why would you need to ride a dragon? You have wings," I say. "How would flying be different than riding a dragon?"

She places the piece of leather on the ground and looks at the blue sky with a dreamy look in her eyes. "A dragon is a creature with such magnificence. I don't like the cruelty that is shown to the dragons either. I have seen how you've bonded with your dragon, and I've heard how your dragon helped to defeat the frost giant that you saved me from. I have many reasons to be thankful for these creatures. I want to change my outlook."

A clatter of rocks sound at the entrance, and as I glance up, I notice Rota has suddenly taken off in a different direction.

- CHAPTER THREE -

That was strange. A small little noise sounds in the corner, and Rota takes off. I have to be cautious of this friendship. I want to believe her intentions, but I'm not quite sure what to think after what she has just said and how she reacted to the noise.

"Where did she go?" Eir stares vacantly at the spot Rota was in only moments before.

I shake my head and toss my arms out from my side with my palms up. "I'm not sure. She might be worried about being caught with us. After all, she was saying how much she had to lose, just like Mistress Sigrun. At the first threat of being discovered, she takes off." I put my leatherwork aside and stand, gazing again at Rota's vacant spot. "It's a strange but nice feeling that she's come to talk to us, but I don't know if I can trust her yet. She's been my archnemesis since day one. She's picked on me every single day. Then suddenly she's changed? I think we should take this one day at a time."

"Maybe she's just working another angle." Hildr's auburn eyebrows knit together as she looks up from her work.

"Trust you to be the negative one, Hildr." Eir shakes her head then flicks her long brown hair over her shoulder.

"I don't know. You might have to be careful. Rota has always had winged Valkyrie mentality through and through. It runs in her family." Britta's brows push into a frown. "Her sister finished at the Valkyrie Academy a couple of years ago, and she was much the same as Rota with her attitude. They do have a lot to lose, and you do need to take it cautiously as Hildr says."

I sit back down and start to work on my spare saddle. "I don't like it, but I understand what you're saying. I like to give people second chances when they deserve it, and I hate to think that there may be a manipulative, underlying reason for the change in attitude."

We start to pack up after several hours of work on the saddles, but another sound on the outskirts of the area interrupts us. A strange uneasiness stirs in my stomach, but I push it away. There's nothing there. It's probably the wind or something else insignificant.

We move away from the tanning area with our saddles almost complete.

I sling my spare saddle over my arm. "We should stop by the dragons and try these on them to see how they fit. We can adjust them from there and then work on the final stages another day."

Hildr shakes out her hands. "My hands are cramping. I don't know how you do this stuff."

"I could do it all the time, Hildr," Eir says. "It's very relaxing."

Hildr shakes her head and screws up her nose, pushing her freckles together. "I find fighting more relaxing."

"Both my hands and arms ache after fighting. I would much rather the stiffness be from creating something." Eir flexes her hands a few times, observing them.

Britta lifts an eyebrow. "Eir, don't you ever think you're in the wrong line of work?"

Genuine confusion etches on Eir's face. "What do you mean?"

Britta tosses her saddle from one arm to the other. "A Valkyrie is supposed to be vicious and always fighting. Yet you always want to be peaceful, and you hate fighting."

"Now that you mention it, I often think that. I wish Valkyries had a peace camp. I'm sure I would get top marks on that one." She fiddles with one of the newly made leather straps on her saddle, turning it over in her hand and admiring the intricate details of the plaits around the edges. Her face lights up. "Perhaps they could make a craft school. That would be peaceful."

We head out of the tanning area with our arms full of the leather goods. As we exit the rock formation, my stomach twitches. Something in the air isn't right. I search the area, trying to work out what's wrong, but I can't place it. The sensation in the air feels like it did before the dark elves arrived, but we got rid of all the dark elves. They should be all gone from Asgard, and they have increased Asgard's security. My search comes up empty. I start to think I'm just imagining things.

Perhaps I'm just feeling Gilroma, but it doesn't seem to match his magic scent, and I don't quite remember the sensation I picked up from the other dark elves before they showed. I shake my head, trying to rid myself of the disconcerted feeling, and we continue to head to the academy.

We enter an area enclosed with large boulders, when suddenly my body is yanked from where it stands and slammed against a boulder. My quiver slightly softens the blow. Something is pressing me hard against it. Nothing visible is holding me, leaving only one other option—an invisible force. I cry out, and my lungs burn. The force is so strong, it is hard for me to recover my breath. My feet dangle in the air as I'm pushed against the hard surface. I feel as though a large vehicle is pressing against me, flattening me against the rock. I attempt to search for my magic and gather it together, but I'm not having much luck. I drag my vision along the ground and lift it to focus on a distant area. Six dark elves approach.

The *oomph* of leather hitting the ground as Hildr drops her saddle draws my attention and is followed by the high-pitched grinding of metal as she draws her sword.

Again, I attempt to break free from the invisible force, but I can't do it. "No," I grunt. I helplessly watch as Hildr approaches the evil force. I need to get out of this and help my friends.

Eir's face blanches, and she drops her saddle, too, before reluctantly reaching for her sword, only to find her hands frozen over its hilt. I'm surprised. This is odd for Eir, even though I know she hates fighting. Perhaps there is another force at play, like the one holding me firmly against this rock.

Britta grabs her sword and pulls it out. I welcome the sound of screaming metal until suddenly it's magically flung from her hand and clangs against a rock. Her eyes widen as they follow the direction of her fleeing sword. "Oh, Vanir!"

Hildr grunts and charges. The elf flicks his hand, and she smashes sideways into a rock. She slumps to the ground, where she lies unmoving. I hope she is only knocked unconscious and nothing worse.

The dark elves move forward in a single line. Excruciatingly, I pull from my magic, but I can't move my arms. I have only mastered the use of magic through my hands and arms. I don't know if there's any other way to use it. We are completely outnumbered by the six elves. I fought against more the other day, but they weren't expecting magic from me, so I had the advantage.

Eir's knees buckle underneath her, and she folds until her bottom sits on top of her heels.

Britta lurches forward, our last line of defense. She stops midstride, her foot poised in the air, her body frozen as an elf concentrates on her.

My hands remain stuck by my sides. It's irking me to watch these dark elves approach us, and there is nothing I can do. I'm dying to call out to Elan except I know that she won't be able to hear me. She would be too far away by now, visiting her mother in the wastelands. I gaze at Hildr, and seeing her like that jerks at my thoughts.

I cry out, "Drogon!" Then my mouth slams shut, and my lips remain fastened together, muffling any other cries. The elves have even used their magic to seal my mouth.

As a dark elf nears, I recognize him as the same one from the other day. The chief of the dark elves's eyes fix solidly on me, and his long, dark leather jacket whips around his ankles as he walks forward. His upper body is covered in dark armor camouflaged over his dark leathers. His long, dark hair flows loosely behind his shoulders, parted by his ears, which point out the sides. When he gets within a few feet of me, his eyes narrow as he observes me stuck against the boulder.

"You disgraced us, young Valkyrie." His voice is full of venom. "What's going to protect you now?" He paces in front of me and continues the motion slowly around the boulder as if stalking his prey. "What's to stop me from ripping you apart, limb by limb, and letting your friends watch?" He cocks an eyebrow as he glances at Hildr then flicks a dismissive hand in her direction. "Except for the one unconscious."

He paces some more, remaining in front of me. "I would love to do that to you, and my colleagues would like to watch." He pauses his pacing and looks at me. "We are a strong race, and you have disgraced us. You have taken from us what is ours. The palace that Odin occupies is meant to be ours." His voice grows louder with each word, and his eyes bulge red as the anger bubbles to an explosive point.

I try hard to pull my hands away from my sides, and I can feel the magic stirring within me, the magic that I desperately want to direct at the elf.

"Let this be a warning." He moves closer to me, and his long fingers stroke under my chin. I flinch, trying to pull away. I can see in his eyes that he has recognized my effort to flinch away. "My main beef is with the winged Valkyries. This time, seeing that you are wingless, I will send you some pity. I believe you are trying to prove a point, but if I give you this chance, I trust that you will not fight against us next time we come. I understand your kind needs to prove yourself against these cruel creatures, the winged Valkyries. And I have always felt a kinship to someone who wields magic." He strokes my chin some more, continuing the motion down my cheek, and I can't help but contort with a shiver. He cocks a dark eyebrow. "No. This will just be a warning. The next time, remember if you go up against us, I will select your friends first and remove their limbs, one by one, in front of you, until eventually, I will work on you. If this is not a deterrence, then I do not know what will be."

He pivots in the opposite direction, and his long, pointy shoes scatter rocks as he walks away from me while leaving me secured to the boulder by his magic. I look at Britta and Eir, and they remain stuck in the same positions, their eyes facing away from me and their bodies rigid. It breaks my heart to see Hildr still unconscious on her side. Her spiky red hair is a bright contrast to the gray rocks.

Flapping sounds behind me in the form of beating wings. A large thump above follows, and my boulder shakes from the force. Above me, a massive roar screeches, followed by a large plume of fire shooting over my head and toward the dark elves. I can't maneuver my face upward even though I am using every effort to search for the instigator of the flame.

A moment later, all of my effort proves wasted. Drogon pushes off the boulder and lands on the ground in front of me. He throws his head forward and roars again at the dark elves, only to be joined by Tanda on his right then Naga on his left. Both of the additional dragons join him by sending out plumes of fire before roaring out smoke. As Drogon throws his head forward again, the elves suddenly disappear.

The three dragons cease their roaring and stare into the distance. Drogon's thoughts meld with our minds. *Where did they go?*

Naga don't know.

Tanda stretches her neck up high, searching the area. I can't see the dark elves anywhere.

Drogon peers over his shoulder and spots Hildr lying flat on the ground. He twists and charges toward her. His nose nuzzles her. *Hildr! Hildr!* He nudges her some more with his nose, and she stirs softly. *Oh, dragon scales! You're okay!* he cries out with excitement in his voice.

Suddenly the magic releases me, and I drop to the ground. "That was close. I can't let that happen again."

- CHAPTER FOUR -

It takes all of my strength to pull myself onto my feet. As soon as I do, I head straight to Hildr. I crumple beside her and lean over her, putting all my weight on my knees. The rough rocks dig into the thin layer of flesh, but I ignore them. "Hildr, are you okay?"

Her green eyes flicker open and gaze at me vaguely, gradually focusing and becoming more alert.

Drogon snorts over the top of us, and her eyes flick up to him. With great effort, she reaches her hand up to him. The big brown dragon moves in, and I lean out, avoiding his many horns. He nudges Hildr softly with his nose. *You had me worried, Hildr. I don't want anything to happen to my Valkyrie.*

Weakly, she strokes his nose and up his snout. "Drogon. Would you miss me?" Her voice is husky.

He pushes her slightly again with his nose. *I have grown rather fond of you.*

"Come on, Hildr. Let's get you up." I offer her my hand.

She grabs one of Drogon's horns and my offered hand, and we pull her up together until she rises to her feet. She lets go of Drogon's horn and stumbles a bit. I tighten my grip on her.

Britta scrambles over. "Here, let me help." She hooks her shoulder underneath Hildr's arm.

Eir pushes me aside and ducks under Hildr's other arm. "I'll take her. You had a bit of a bashing back there."

I release Hildr to Eir's care and drop back with Drogon. "Did you hear me call you, Drogon?"

His dark-brown eyes are serious as he nods once. *It was faint, but yes, I did hear you. Before Elan left, she told me to keep an eye on you.*

"Thank you, Drogon." I stoop down, pick up the saddles, and throw them over my arms. They are heavier than I anticipated, dragging me down on my left side. I do my best to ignore the strain.

They look too heavy for you, Kara. Let me take them to my stall, and you can come and collect them later.

"Would you do that, Drogon?"

I'm not fond of saddles, as I don't like the idea of being restrained, but I like the idea of making my Valkyrie safe on my back. Hildr is a bit of a daredevil, but I don't want to lose her off my back. I would feel guilty for the rest of my life. It would kill me inside, knowing that I had options for keeping her safe and didn't use them.

"Thank you." I gaze over at Tanda. "How is she doing? Is she settling in with this idea okay?"

She is a little more apprehensive than I was when I first started.

I smile. "You were rather apprehensive. It took Hildr over a day to coax you into letting her touch you."

He clears his throat. *Yes, well, Tanda is a bit more touchy because she has been treated worse than I was. I also had a little bit of time with you when you cleaned out my stall.* He glances over at Tanda, his eyes thoughtful. *For some reason, the Valkyries aren't dragging Naga and me out to fight. I am hoping this will extend to Tanda also. I don't know if something has happened or why they leave us alone. Maybe somebody is working on the other side to stop the Valkyries from dragging us out because they always like to try out the new dragons.*

"I don't know. Perhaps Eingana sorted something out when she came to visit Odin that time after he kidnapped Elan. She didn't disclose everything that was in that visit." I place the saddles on the ground, and Drogon picks one up then looks at Tanda and Naga. They come running over and grab a saddle each.

He looks at me. *Do you think you'll be okay? I can't see any more dark elves.*

"I can't sense them at the moment either. I think they might be gone. They said they were only trying to threaten me. Then you arrived, and they seemed to disappear. So we should be fine. Thank you so much for showing up."

That's okay. But if I didn't, I would have been dead meat in Elan's eyes. I would never have heard the end of it. But that's not the only reason I came. He glances at Hildr.

"Well, thanks again."

The three dragons push off into the air, and I watch them disappear back to the stalls. I turn around to see Eir and Britta still helping Hildr. They have managed to travel a fair distance. I jog quickly to reach them. "Are you guys okay?"

"Yeah, we're fine." Eir peers over her shoulder at me. "We're going to take her to see the healer. I think Anita should see her just to be sure."

"Good idea. If you're okay, then I'm going to take off and take care of something."

Eir frowns, and her eyes are full of concern. "Sure. But be careful. Okay? Those elves came out of nowhere, and I'd hate them to attack you again while you're by yourself. Not that we would be much help." She looks slightly embarrassed.

I shake my head. "Don't worry. It's not your fault. They hit us early, and I should have recognized the warning signs. I can sense their magic, but I can't sense it now."

"Okay then. Maybe you should pay better attention next time. I would hate to have something happen to you." Eir notices my empty arms. "Where are all the saddles?"

"The dragons took them back to the stalls. They were too heavy for me to carry them all, and Drogon offered to take them back. We can grab them later."

"Great. That's an excellent idea. Take care then, okay?"

"Okay." I spin around and run in the opposite direction, making sure that I head toward the academy. The last thing I need is for them to follow me, not only because I want to keep my secret, but also because Hildr needs a healer's attention. When I'm confident that I'm alone, I run straight for Gilroma's cave. I haven't seen him since the attack of the dark elves, and now questions burn inside of me.

I run down the dark, thin tunnel. It has lost all eeriness since I have been here so many times. Instead, trying to get to the far end is an inconvenience. He has buried himself so deep in this mountain. I barge into his little cave and notice that he has made use of the second room that I created while practicing using my magic. He has even created a small bed on the far side. Before, the cave had piles of rocks everywhere and looked extremely unhospitable. The strange elven figurines are spread out and appear more decorative than just placed inside, and he has decorated the walls with strange painted markings. By luck, the dark elf is sitting inside the cave, and he glances up from a book he is studying while stirring the pot that's boiling over a small fire.

"Kara! It's been a while. Why do you look so worried?" His glowing yellow eyes assess my body, and his nose twitches. "I can smell magic." He places his book to the side and stands. "Are you okay? I can smell your fear and apprehension."

"I wasn't okay. We were attacked by six elves that were in the attack of the other day. I'm sure you must have heard about it or at least sensed it."

His hairless eyebrow rises. "Yes. I did hear about the elves and the attack the other day. And I heard that you did wonders with your magic."

"How do you hear of these things all the time? You're always hiding in this cave. I never see you outside of it. So how do you hear about all the news?"

A strange smirk spreads across his face. "I have my ways."

I raise an eyebrow and cross my arms, leaning to one side. "It's going to be like that, is it?"

"That's the best way to have it." His eyes twinkle with mischief. "Why, what happened today?"

"Six of the dark elves came back somehow. I don't know how, and they just disappeared later. But one was the main elf from the other day, and he was specifically looking for me. What is worse is that he and his comrades also attacked my friends."

His eyes turn serious, and his brows push together into a frown. "Why didn't you protect them or yourself with your magic?"

"He didn't give me a chance. He tainted their magic somehow, making it hard for me to detect since I've had such little exposure to their magic. The sensation was different from the other day. I didn't recognize it immediately, and it was too late by the time he hit me and pinned me against a boulder with his magic. I couldn't move my arms. It stopped me from doing anything with my magic. He then attacked my friends and threatened all of us, and I couldn't do anything about it." I rub my temples, straining over the horror of the memory. "They told me that if I use magic against them again and stop them from doing what they want, they will rip my friends' limbs off one by one in front of me and then they will work on me."

Gilroma approached me and stroked my upper arm. "That's terrible. Are you okay?"

I toss my head to look in the opposite direction. "I'm okay, but I feel vulnerable. It frustrates me that I couldn't use my magic because my arms were pinned to my side before I knew what was happening. It frustrates me that I'm the only one with the magic and my friends have nothing. Why couldn't the zmey have marked them as well? At least then everything wouldn't rely on me, and more of us would have magic. I know my friends have good hearts. They would always protect Asgard. So why couldn't the zmey pick them, too, and not just me?"

Something flicks through the dark elf's eyes, and they dart to the corner. I follow his gaze, and my eyes land on the pile of books. Perhaps he is thinking of some passage in these books to use as a reference.

He looks back at me. "That's an interesting thought."

I look deep into his glowing eyes, and a thought suddenly occurs to me. "Gilroma? Your eyes are bright yellow and glow, but the other elves' eyes were dark and evil. Why are yours so different?"

He removes his hand from my upper arm and paces in front of me in a small circle. "There is a lot about me that you do not know. My past is tainted with so many things, and some you may not like."

I frown at him. "I would not think any differently of you. Perhaps one day you will tell me."

"Perhaps. Maybe one day."

- CHAPTER FIVE -

Try as I might, I can't use the magic any other way than with my hands. I work relentlessly alongside Gilroma and try over and over again, yet it won't manifest any other way. I slump forward in defeat. "I just can't do it," I moan as my energy bleeds from me, making my head woozy.

I sit on the stone seat and lean my head back against the hard rock wall inside his cave.

Gilroma runs his hands over the trident-shaped tattoo on his bald forehead and paces the room. His movements cause his leather clothes to squeak. Small rocks scatter across the hard surface of the floor as his shoes clip them in their travels. He sighs deeply, goes to a corner, and digs out a box I haven't seen before. He removes the lid and digs through its contents. Eventually, he pulls his hand out, accidentally knocking it against the side. A slight clang rings out. A long chain droops through his fingers, following his hand out of the box. He opens his hand, exposing a necklace lying in his palm. Awkwardly, his big fingers track down the links and fiddle with the clasp before unhinging it. He walks toward me and hooks his arms around my neck then secures the clasp together behind my neck and lets the necklace droop over my chest. Instantly, I grasp the ornament between my fingers and study it. Lying in the middle of the metal shape is a large blue stone that forms an upside-down raindrop. I rub the shiny surface between the threads of silver that secure it in place.

"What's this?" I turn it around so I can look at it properly.

"It's a necklace charmed with magic. It helps draw your magic together and helps you control it. I fear your magic is not settling in well with your body, and I think it might need a little help."

I stroke my thumb over the stone a couple more times. "I love it. Thank you."

Kara! Elan's voice telepathically speaks to me. *Kara! Where are you?*

Hearing Elan rejuvenates my energy, and I stand quickly, nearly knocking Gilroma in the head. "Oh, sorry!"

He steps away from me. "What's going on?" He frowns, and his chin pushes out, accentuating the spiky tattoos along his jawline.

"Elan just called out to me. She sounds worried, so I better go. I'll see you later." Without waiting for a response, I head out the door and down the long, eerie tunnel without looking back. I am confident that his glowing yellow eyes are watching me. A cool breeze blows from behind me, and I charge down the long tunnel.

Kara! Where are you? Elan calls again.

As I charge out of the tunnel, a shadow circles overhead. I glance up to see Elan flying over the top of me. "I'm here!" I call up to her. "Directly under you."

She tilts her head and looks down. *Oh, thank dragon scales! You had me so worried.* She angles down to land, and when she hits the ground, a few rocks scatter aside. She stomps forward, shoving her nostrils in front of my face. *Where have you been? I've been searching for you everywhere. Drogon told me what happened. Are you all right? I can't leave you for a moment!*

I chuckle and stroke the side of her face. "I'm fine, Elan. Stop worrying. Drogon had it covered. He, Naga, and Tanda did a wonderful job of protecting us."

They got there too late. If they were a second later, it would have been bad. Her golden eyes fix on me, sharp with stress.

"I don't know. I don't think the dark elves were really going to do anything that bad, although it was scary. I think their visit was more of a threat."

They still could have hurt you, you know.

"I'm fine, Elan! Really, I am. Stop worrying. Although I can't believe you're back so soon. Have you finished relaying everything to your mother?"

I have.

"And?"

She sits on her haunches and lifts her chin. *Well, she's quite proud of me. She says I've been doing a good job and was quite impressed that the dragons are coming over slowly to work with the wingless Valkyries. She doesn't expect them to work with the winged Valkyries. That would be a contradiction to their beliefs.*

"That's true. I wouldn't expect the dragons to forgive the winged Valkyries quickly."

Elan tilts her head to the side. *Where have you been, anyway? I've looked everywhere for you, and I couldn't see you anywhere from the sky.*

"I've been visiting Gilroma."

Who?

"Gilroma," I repeat, looking at her strangely. Then it dawned on me. "Oh. I haven't told you about him, have I? He's the one who has been helping me use my magic."

She searches the area with her eyes. *Where is he?*

"He's down that tunnel." I turn to point at the entrance, only to be startled by something flying quickly out of the tunnel. I watch the creature fly away.

Is that a bat?

"I don't know. I didn't know there were bats down the tunnel. That's where Gilroma lives. Down there."

Elan stares at it and frowns, the scales above her head bunching together. *That's a strange place for someone to be.*

"I know. But he's not exactly normal for Asgard."

What do you mean?

I balk before I say, "He's a dark elf."

A dark elf? Her voice booms in my head. *I haven't seen any around other than the ones that attacked the other day. Are you sure he's trustworthy?* She stomps over to the tunnel and sniffs the entrance. *He smells familiar.* She turns back to me, her face wearing a look of confusion. *Have I met him before?*

"No. I don't believe you have."

She turns back and sniffs the entrance again, this time more loudly, and I can hear her snorting. *The smell is very familiar. I have definitely smelled him before. I just can't place my talon on where.* She turns back to me. *Can I meet him?*

"I don't see why not, but there's no way you are going to fit down this tunnel. I'll have to see if he'll come out. Wait here. It's quite a long tunnel, so be patient. Okay?"

She nods once.

I work my way back down the tunnel, and I can hear Elan's breathing following me. She's still snorting the air, taking in every scent that travels along the wind. Eventually, I reach the end of the tunnel and follow the flickering the lights into the caves that I had left only moments before. But I can't see Gilroma.

I go into the room that I created the other day and see that his bed remains neatly made, but the place is empty. I go back out to the main room and stare at the pot still boiling over the fire. He's gone, but I don't know how.

Puzzled, I stand in the middle of the room. I can't for the life of me think of how he left without Elan or me seeing him go. Completely baffled, I exit the cave and head back down the tunnel toward Elan's eyes staring at me from the far end.

I don't see him. The golden dragon squints. *Why are you coming out alone, Kara?*

I stop in front of her nose. "He's completely gone. I don't know where he went. Did you see anyone coming out of the cave when we were talking before?"

She shakes her head.

- CHAPTER SIX -

That's a shame. I'm keen to meet this Gilroma. I want to see if he is good for you.

"Aww. What's this? Are you acting like a mother to me now?" I poke Elan's leg.

Someone's got to do it. You certainly don't know how to look after yourself—always getting into trouble when I turn my back.

"Oh, whatever." I nudge her with my elbow, and she nudges me back with the side of her head. I stumble over a rock and land against the hard surface of the tunnel wall.

Elan looks down the tunnel. *What sort of place is this to live anyway? It's so sheltered and in the middle of nowhere.*

"Let's just say he's an unusual character, and he wouldn't fit in very well with most Asgardians. If you were a strange character, you wouldn't fit in very well with Asgardians either, and you would probably hide in the middle of a mountain."

Aren't I already an unusual character who most Asgardians don't like? She tilts her head to the side. *Even so, I wouldn't hide in some cave buried deep within a mountain. That's way too claustrophobic.*

I frown. "True. But you're very large and would be a formidable opponent to anyone who challenges you. Plus, you have wings."

Kind of different, but not really. I still wouldn't hide inside a cave. She screws up her nose, and her scales clump together.

"Yeah, I can't stand the cave so deep inside the mountain either. I'm always afraid that it will collapse on top of me, especially when I use my magic inside of it."

Suddenly, Elan's face turns serious, and she tilts her head to the side. *What is that?*

I look in the same direction, unable to spot anything. "What's what?"

She ignores me, and the strange look remains on her face. She tilts her head in the other direction.

"Elan, what's what?" I ask again. I stand next to her and rest my hand on her side.

Quick, get on! She squats her front legs, making it easier for me to climb on. It's harder to secure myself without the saddle on her back. I wrap my legs around her neck and clasp the scales at the front with my hands. She pushes off into the air. We rise slowly, my body rocking up and down as her wings labor to lift us. She has me worried, and I can feel the frown adding pressure to my forehead.

Without a word, she flies a short distance before descending again. It is then that I see it, and the depths of my stomach churn with deep, aching pain.

I spot the zmey hovering over something on the ground then dive toward a moving object. On the ground, three figures are scattering to the sides. The zmey drops, claws first, striking the pale-faced Valkyrie. It then flaps its wings, rising in the air, and dives for another. My cheeks turn clammy as the blood runs from my face. It is attacking Hildr, Eir, and Britta.

A glint catches my eye, and I spot a sword lying on the ground a few feet away from where my friends are standing. Hildr dashes for it but gets knocked down by the zmey. It drags its talons down her back, tearing her leather uniform, before knocking the sword out of her reach. Her cry cuts the air, followed by Eir's scream, as the zmey dives toward her and scratches her as well. Britta charges off in one direction, leaving me puzzled, until I realize there is also a sword lying not far from her. The zmey swoops down, blocking her from the weapon, and aims for her. It drags its claws down her torso, managing to catch her arm at the same time.

"Quick, Elan," I call.

She lands with a thud, and the ground shudders underneath her. I throw my leg over her neck and slide off her back. Dirt swooshes around me as she pumps her wings and returns to the sky. *I'll get you, you rotten little creature. I'll teach you for stealing our eggs and attacking my friends.* She darts for the zmey, and its small body maneuvers quickly to the side, out of the way.

I dive for a sword and race back to Hildr. I make sure she's okay then help her to her feet and hand her the sword. Some relief washes over me when I see that the gashes aren't too deep, but I know from experience that they hurt.

Elan lunges for the zmey again, her threats continuing. *Come here, you slimy little creature. I would love to teach you a lesson.*

The zmey dives for Elan from the side, and Elan struggles momentarily with her large body, trying to stop herself from flopping forward. Using this opportunity, the zmey pushes up and disappears around the edge of a mountain. As soon as Elan steadies herself, she pursues the zmey, trying to catch the trail before it turns cold. It takes her a moment to launch her massive form into the air and steady her wings.

The zmey appears briefly before completely disappearing, and Elan fades into invisibility.

I head toward Britta and help her stand before leading her to her sword. Then I move to help Eir. Britta has gashes all down her stomach and on the inside of her arm. Eir doesn't look much better, with gashes all along her shoulders and down her arm.

Eir places her hand over one of her wounds. "What just happened? Why is the zmey attacking us? What did we do?"

I feel a deep tinge of guilt growing through my body. It was only a short time before that I mentioned to Gilroma how I wished the zmey would mark my friends so they could have magic and help me out. Looking at their state, I don't know what I was thinking. Even so, I don't understand why the zmey would suddenly attack my friends. That was a private conversation buried deep within a mountain. No one could have heard us, let alone Loki.

"Other than a few gashes, are you all feeling okay?" It takes a considerable effort to push the guilt aside, even though I was only thinking out loud about this happening. I didn't cause it.

"A little shaken up." Britta slides her sword back into its sheath. "And feeling a little sorry for myself. Besides that, I feel all right."

"I feel the same." Hildr flinches as she reaches for her back. "But I'd love to know why the zmey decided to attack us."

"Does that mean we've been marked with magic?" Eir asks. "Was that the creature that marked you, Kara?"

I nod then get distracted by a roar that echoes through the valley. I search for Elan but can't see her. She must still be invisible. I can't see the zmey either. I focus back on Eir. "I'm not sure. I'm not sure if the zmey has marked you with magic. But if it did, wouldn't that be a good thing?"

Hildr's eyebrows tweak with interest. "Is that a possibility?"

"It's the same creature that marked me and created the magic inside of me. But it's also Loki in one of his many images."

Britta looks at me in disbelief. "You mean Loki would do this?"

"That's what I've been told and what I've read. I have read that that creature is Loki and that when he marks you, it is a mark of magic and eventually you will manifest the power. I shrug. That's pretty much what happened to me anyway."

Elan's golden form appears from around the corner, flying in our direction.

"Don't tell Elan that the creature is Loki, though," I whisper. "At least until I work out that it is Loki for certain. I'll fill you in on the rest later."

Elan lands, and the ground shakes. Her face is etched with annoyance. *It disappeared again. I want to tear that little creature apart. It's been stealing our eggs, and I still can't get to it. Did you see where it went?* She looks at us individually. The three of us shake our heads.

"No. Sorry, Elan. I didn't see it. I would tell you if I did," I say.

She huffs and throws her head to the side. *I'm going to search again.* And with that, she pushes off into the air. The dust billows up around us as her wings flap toward the ground.

I look at my three friends. "It would be best if you get your wounds attended to. If you're ready for another shock, I know someone who can achieve this properly."

They stare at me blankly. My skin crawls, but I don't blame them. They are getting bombarded with a lot of shocks at once.

Hesitantly, I ask, "Are you ready for another shock?"

- CHAPTER SEVEN -

"What do you mean another shock?" Hildr's eyes are wide, and she points in the direction that the zmey flew, even though it's out of sight. "We've just been scratched by that zmey creature. What other sorts of shock do you have for us?"

I shrug and fiddle with my hands in front of me. "There's someone else I've been seeing."

The words come out quickly, and I suddenly feel the need to study the ground.

"Do you mean that angel of death?" Eir's voice rises with excitement.

"Yes." Then I register what she said. I look up and shake my head. "I mean, no. Not like that, Eir." I frown at her. "How did Harut come into this?"

She shrugs. "I don't know. You're the one who's talking about secrets."

"I'm talking about something else." I huff with exasperation and take turns looking at my friends. "Come with me. There's only one way to do this."

I head back in the direction I came. I can't help but notice how clear and blue the sky looks, absent of golden dragons and the zmey. Elan hasn't returned, so I can only imagine that she hasn't caught up with the zmey yet and remains in her invisible form to pursue it.

I lead my friends back to Gilroma's place, listening to their confused comments and winces over the pain they are feeling from the scratches. At least I know from experience that their wounds are not deadly. We enter the long, thin tunnel.

"Where are you taking us, Kara? This place is creepy!" Britta's voice sounds on edge.

I turn around and face them, barely making out their eyes in the dim glow of the distant light from the candles. "I'm not sure if he is going to be here, but if he is, he should be able to help with your scars and your healing."

Britta pulls at her leather clothes, trying to pull her shirt over the top of her wound.

"Just a word of warning, though. He's a bit of a strange creature," I say.

Hildr grunts. "What do you mean that he is a creature? Haven't we had enough strange creatures for the day?"

I lift my hand in a stopping motion. "Just bear with me. He's helped me out a lot with my magic, but he has to be kept a secret. So please, keep this secret." I clasp my hands together. "If you don't, then my trainer of magic will disappear forever. He is the one that taught me how to raise the barriers that helped us against the dark elves."

They nod in unison and follow me down the dingy tunnel. Their footsteps echo loudly through the thin, enclosed alleyway. Finally, I reach the light at the end of the tunnel and circle around into the room. I'm surprised to see Gilroma is back and sitting in his usual spot.

I move farther into the room. "Where were you before?"

His glowing eyes lift from his book and observe me. "What do you mean?"

"Elan wanted to meet you, so I came back in straight after I left, but somehow you sneaked past me."

He shrugs his shoulders. "I just went out for a quick errand, but I'm back now. And you're back so soon? What a strange surprise!"

"I brought some friends. They need your help." His face turns pale, and his glowing eyes seem to burn right through me. Suddenly, I'm questioning my decision. "I hope this okay."

"I don't know. It depends on who they are. And are they going to keep my location a secret? You say 'friends.' How many?" His voice is low and grumbling.

"Just a few. I trust them, and they promised to keep you and your place a secret."

He nods once.

I turn around and call my friends. "Come on, guys! You can come around." I unstrap my weapons and rest them in the nearest corner.

Hildr comes around the corner first, and her jaw clenches as her gaze crosses the cave. "Isn't he a dark elf?"

Eir comes around the corner, and Britta follows close behind. Her eyes widen as she stares at Gilroma's glowing yellow eyes.

"Yes, he is a dark elf. Remember, I said that he helped me channel my magic, which helped to stop the dark elves that invaded us? He also helped after the zmey marked me again after the initial mark on my shoulder. Come in and let him take a look at your wounds."

Apprehensively, they enter the cave together.

"Clearly we have to work on our trust issues in this little group," I say. "I trust Gilroma, and I trust you guys. We just have to learn to trust each other. You could get him to look at those wounds. Perhaps he can heal them enough so that you're not left with big, nasty scars. Gilroma healed my last wound from the zmey until the scar completely disappeared."

Hildr lets out an exasperated sigh. "Scars never worried me, but what the heck? Here." She stands in front of him, and he observes her strangely.

Eventually, he stands and reaches for his ointment. "This can sting a little." He dips his fingers in the ointment, and his hand pauses not far from her body. "And I have to touch you."

"I can put it on." Hildr reaches for the ointment.

He yanks the jar away. "Not if you want it to heal properly. It has to come from my fingers." A sad resignation fills his voice.

"Fine, then." She faces away, exposing her sore to him by lifting the flap of her torn clothes. She hisses as he gently runs his ointment-covered fingers along the wound.

He does this a few times before pulling his hand back. "There. That should do."

Hildr reaches around and feels the area of her skin under the torn leather. Her fingers tap the area as though searching in a panic. "There's nothing there."

"No. It's healed." Gilroma wipes his fingers on a cloth, ridding them of the salve.

"Thank you," she says stiffly, as though remembering who she is talking to and pushing away her excitement.

Eir charges up to Gilroma. "I'm next."

He smiles. "Of course. The peaceful one."

Eir balks, and her face flattens in shock. "How do you know that?"

"Kara talks about you all the time."

Eir glances at me. "Really?"

He shakes his head, unable to hold back his smile. "No… And yes. But to be honest, I can smell it on you. You're a peacemaker, and that is what I live for." He runs his salve-covered fingers along her wound.

She squeals slightly and gazes at Hildr. "That really does hurt, doesn't it?"

Seeing Gilroma is finished with Eir, Britta apprehensively approaches. "I guess I'm next." She lifts the torn leather away from her torso and watches him intensely as he works, hissing when he puts the cream on her wound.

Within moments, he pulls back. "There. It should be all done.

She reaches down and feels for the sore with her fingers. "That's a miracle!"

He chuckles. "I wouldn't call it that." He shrugs. "But if that's what you really want to name it…"

Eir looks down at Britta's torso. "There's not a single scar in sight." Her eyes soften when she looks at him. "You must be a miracle worker. Not even Anita could heal it like this."

Gilroma moves to the corner and puts his ointment away. "I'm flattered."

Hildr narrows her eyes at him. "So what are you doing in here, so deep in the mountain? Since when have you lived in Asgard?"

His eyes widen for a moment as he looks at her, and he sucks in his scarred cheeks. Then he relaxes and nods. "I guess all these questions are to be expected. I am a friend of Anita's, and I've been here for many, many years. Recently, I've worked with Kara. She was directed here by your healer."

"Really?" Hildr's eyes are still squinting. "Anita has never mentioned you."

"Yes. Anita is good like that. I have asked her not to mention me unless it is deemed necessary. She has kept her word. And I'll ask the same of you. If you want me to help you with your magic, you must keep my space a secret. I do not believe Odin will tolerate me living here." His eyes suddenly grow a bit brighter.

"How come your eyes glow?" Hildr leans forward to get a closer look.

"The elves we saw the other day had brown eyes." Eir sounds slightly embarrassed over Hildr's lack of kindness.

"That is a long story," he says as he looks at us one by one. "Now, let's see what you can do with your magic."

- CHAPTER EIGHT -

I leave Gilroma's cave feeling elated and confused. My two best friends, Hildr and Eir, and my newest friend, Britta, have been tainted with magic. The zmey decided to mark them, and this confuses me, but at the same time, I'm happy that they have been given the gift of magic. Their powers are already manifesting under Gilroma's guidance, and they have only been marked for a short period. At the same time, I don't understand why the zmey has marked them. I wonder why it has suddenly picked on my friends and not the other Valkyries.

I need to find Loki. My mind whirls with thoughts and ideas of where I might be able to find him. All of them are eventually leading back to the palace. Perhaps I should try there. Loki must be somewhere close if he has just appeared as the zmey again and was on the hill when the dark elves attacked and the senior Valkyries came to help.

"I'm beat!" Hildr's shoulders slump. "How do you do it all the time?"

"I'm exhausted too." Eir's face is a lighter shade than usual. "Now I know how you felt when you passed out before."

"I'm going to have a shower and get cleaned up." Britta runs a hand over her blood-soaked leathers, attempting to cover her torso. "I seriously need to find new leathers. If Mistress Sigrun finds us, she is not going to be impressed, and if she presses us for answers, she's going to be even less impressed knowing that we have been marked with magic."

"That's an understatement. I'm coming too." Hildr screws up her nose at her clothes. "I feel disgusting, and I'm exhausted."

"What are you going to do, Kara?" Eir asks.

"I'm going to wander around for a bit, I think. I'm so happy you guys have magic, too, but I'm also a little confused. I need to clear my head and think it over."

"Don't go doing anything stupid," Britta says.

I give her a strange look. "Gee, thanks, Britta."

"You know what I mean," she says.

"Yeah, but if she does, then she won't have us by her side to help protect her with magic," Hildr says.

I roll my eyes. "I'll try and keep out of trouble. Okay?"

Eir lifts her eyebrow at me. "Good. So we'll see you soon?"

I smile innocently. "Of course. I have to get to class soon anyway." We part ways, and I watch them slowly walk away as they receive strange glances from the guards around the academy. With the torn clothes and no wounds, they are an odd sight.

When I'm confident that they're gone, I head straight for the palace, sneaking past the area where Elan likes to sleep. I don't know if she is lying invisible or if she's just not there, but I don't want to upset her by letting her know where I'm going. I still don't think it's a good idea to let her go near Odin, just in case he doesn't honor his word and captures her again. There's something about his promises that I don't trust. And I know that he wants an emperor dragon as another marking that he is the most powerful god on Asgard.

Dark clouds gather across the sky, and I can't shake the eerie feeling that something terrible is going to happen, especially when the clouds cover the sun, sending the land into a darker shade. I trek around the mountains and finally spot Odin's castle in the distance. Suddenly, an enormous crack of thunder rumbles across the sky, and the sky responds by releasing the walls held within the clouds. Rain falls without reprieve, drenching my clothes and my path. Puddles slosh around my shoes, soaking them until my feet slip over their inner lining.

A large crack of thunder rumbles again, and I start to wonder if Odin has gotten wind of what I'm expecting to do. Although I can't understand why he would care if I visit Loki. Perhaps he has been annoyed by someone else, and Odin is getting Thor to send out a message that all of Asgard can hear. Or maybe it is just the weather. I approach the castle and see the guards standing close to the main entrance, trying to escape the rain. This could be problematic. It may be harder to sneak past them.

I duck under the canopy of a nearby building and study them, wondering what to do but at the same time trying to look inconspicuous. One of the guard's eyes land on me, and he watches me for a moment before getting distracted and looking elsewhere. In some ways, I wish I'd brought Elan. She might have been able to distract them or help me sneak in. In another way, I'm glad that I didn't. I would hate to put Elan in danger for such a small reason.

I decide to bite the bullet, so I charge up to the front door and approach the guards directly. I skim the palace steps two at a time.

"Halt!" the guard on the right calls out as I bound up the last step.

I gaze at his name embroidered on his top near the shoulder. "Please, Gorm, I just want to get out of this rain. I beg of you, let me past." I put on the most distressed look I can muster and flutter my eyes innocently for a few beats.

Gorm lifts his nose. "You know the only people allowed past this area into the castle are members of the staff or people invited by Odin or one of the royal occupants."

"But it's pouring out here." I hold my hands over my head in a wasted attempt to stop the drops from falling on my head. I can feel the rain saturating my clothes. As a last attempt, I dart forward and stand in line with the guards. Instantly, their spears crisscross in front of me in a combined movement, blocking my path. I raise my hands in defeat. "Okay, okay. I'm stopping right here. I wasn't entering the castle. I was only getting out of the rain."

"We have already discussed this. You can't get any farther unless you have an invitation from one of the royal members or you work here." The guard on the left glares down at me. "The rain excuse is invalid. I saw you taking shelter in that building down there. You could have stayed there."

He's right. I did see him watching me before, but I had to try. My mind races with scenarios that may persuade them to let me in. One idea intrigues me. "I do have an invitation, Birger."

Birger's eyebrow rises. "Really? And who is it from?" His mouth thins to a line of disbelief.

"I have an invitation from Loki." I know it's a desperate move, but it's worth a try.

The two guards double over at the waist. A burst of deep, roaring laughter bellows as they hold their stomachs.

"That's hilarious," Gorm says through fits of laughter. It takes all of Birger's strength to regain his composure, and he stands straight. His mouth remains tilted up at the corners, and he struggles to retain the giggles. "Any royal person other than Loki? You will need an invitation from anybody but Loki."

I frown. "Why? I received an invitation from Loki. He's one of the gods and members of the palace."

Gorm stands straight, just managing to hold back his laughter, yet a chuckle escapes through his words. "Loki is a mischief-maker, and anybody invited by Loki is also regarded in such manner."

I cross my arms over my chest. "Well, I'm not up to mischief. Loki requested to see me, so I was trying to fulfill that request."

Birger speaks. "Go home, Valkyrie. If you really want to enter the castle, then work on your career and make that your dream. You are a servant to the gods and other Valkyries, so work hard and learn how to scrub to perfection, and you may be assigned to the castle in the future. That is the only way you'll be able to enter."

I face him directly. My ears are ringing with his insult, and my eyes narrow. "Yes, I am a

Valkyrie of the wingless kind. But I'm worth more than what you give me credit for."

"Ah. So you're that Valkyrie," Gorm says. "Then you're definitely not allowed to enter the castle." He shrugs. "Odin's orders."

Birger nods. "Yup. That's right. Odin's orders."

"In fact, Odin said to arrest you if you come anywhere near the castle," Gorm says.

My jaw drops. "What?"

He doesn't answer me. Instead, Birger grabs me from behind and secures my wrists. Then Gorm grabs me by the shoulders, and they both direct me inside and down the hallway.

- CHAPTER NINE -

My plodding, reluctant steps echo against the walls of the palace. I slam each foot down while applying a slight backward pressure, making it harder for the guards to drag me down the corridor. At the same time, I know I don't have any other choice but to go with them.

Suddenly, I wish that I had told Elan or one of my friends where I was going. Elan would again accuse me of always getting myself into trouble, and I'm starting to think that she's right. No matter what I do, I always land under the disagreeable eye of the gods or the senior Valkyries.

Roughly, I'm dragged down the hall until, finally, we reach Odin's large throne room. The two guards bang through the door, opening it without knocking. Odin stands behind his throne, and he glowers over his shoulder at the disturbance.

"What is the meaning of this?" His voice rumbles deeply as he spins around the back of his throne, and his one eye focuses on me. The wrinkles around his eye tightens as he observes the way that the guards are handling me. "Oh. This is a sufficient reason. Bring her in."

Birger and Gorm struggle to drag me deeper inside the room. Each of my steps is placed in a breaking position, revealing my apprehension about going any farther inside the room. They give me a final shove forward, and Odin slowly paces around his throne to the front. His gaze doesn't waver from me as he sits in a slow, decisive manner. He rubs his hand through his graying beard then rests his fingers on the armrest of the throne. His face portrays many expressions as the great god stares at me.

Removing his vision from me, he looks at the two guards. "Guards, you must return to your posts. Be cheerful. You have done well. There are enough guards in here to secure this Valkyrie."

The guards nod, release me from their grasp, and abruptly leave. His statement makes me want to pull out my magic and harm a thing or two, but I refrain from doing this. I don't know if Odin is capable of such magic, and I don't want to seem like I think I'm superior because I have magic.

Standing alone in front of the throne, I shake out my arms, releasing the pressure applied to them from the guards' hold. "Why am I here, great Odin?"

Odin raises his chin and stares down at me. "You must show me respect, young Valkyrie."

I expel a loud sigh. "Yes, yes. I must show you respect." I hear the defiance in my voice, and I rein it in. I have to watch my mouth more carefully when it comes to my seniors. I bow my head slightly. "And I do. Although it would be a much easier feat if you would treat us fairly, great Odin." I cringe inwardly. I can still hear the spitefulness tainting my voice, even if it is mild.

"There you go again. You are showing me disrespect and speaking out of line." Odin clicks his fingers. "I will not put up with such insolence. I will not tolerate such disrespect."

My shoulders sag. "Great Odin, I have heard that you show respect to people who stand up for Asgard and fight for its safety."

"Yes, I do. Naturally." He shuffles his backside onto his throne.

"Then why don't you respect me and show me a little bit of respect?" I labor hard to keep my tone courteous.

He leans forward, resting his elbows on the throne's armrests. "Why would you deserve respect?"

"Because I have fought for Asgard. Have you not heard? Have you not seen with your all-seeing eye, as you sit there on your throne and gaze across the land?"

Odin frowns and flicks his hands dismissively at me until eventually, his frown lightens. "Oh, you mean all those discussions of you running around and disobeying your mistress and the rules of Asgard?"

"Is that all that she's said I've done?" I stare at him in disbelief. "Is that how you view it, even though I have done great things to protect Asgard?"

"Protect it? That is a far cry from what I understand you've been doing."

"But I have helped protect Asgard from the dark elves and a giant. I have stood up against all the odds to protect Asgard. That is how I see it. Not how you've described it."

"You attacked Mistress Sigrun and her group of Valkyries, hindering them from learning how to fight against the dragons."

"Do you mean the one time that I stopped them from attacking a dragon and hurting it for no reason? Because I'm not going to hurt a dragon, and you shouldn't want to hurt them either. They have also helped save Asgard. Because of my friendship with them, they have stood by our sides and helped us fight against the dark elves, just like my dragon, Elan, did when we fought against the frost giant. You should be treating the dragons with respect. They have an intelligence that is beyond your comprehension."

His brows push together. "Are you saying I'm dumb?" He slams his fist down on his armrest. "I am the god of wisdom. I am not unintelligent. How dare you accuse me of such."

I bow my head slightly. "Great Odin, I was not implying that you are unintelligent. As you said, you are the god of wisdom. I was merely saying that the dragons hold a great intelligence that you are not yet aware of, even in your great wisdom." The words drag out of my mouth. I must try to flatter Odin. I am only going to win this battle if he is on my side, and I need him on my side.

The god's eye narrows as he stares at me. "Flattery will not get you anywhere, young Valkyrie."

I swallow the contents of my stomach and do my best to make my voice sound convincing. "I'm not flattering you, great Odin. I'm merely stating the truth."

His face seems to soften a little.

So I continue. "I was only working in the interest of Asgard even if you saw it as me being rebellious. I am trying to prove my worth and the worth of my comrades, the other wingless Valkyries. We are willing to fight for Asgard and do more than become servants."

He frowns. "But you also fought against the winged Valkyries, and I hear that you defied them on that mountaintop while using magic."

"I wasn't given a choice but to participate in that fight. It was supposed to be three wingless Valkyries against three winged Valkyries, except the fight proved to be unfair because all the winged Valkyries from the academy were fighting against only three wingless Valkyries—myself and my two wingless friends. When the fight turned unfair, my magic unleased itself out of pure defense. Plus, I wanted to earn the right to go to Midgard and save the souls of the great warriors for Valhalla, a quest that I have since learned is only granted by your greatness. I was hoping that since I've been so faithful to Asgard and have proved myself, that you would also grant me the ability to reap souls for Valhalla. I heard it is done by your touch."

Odin's laughter is deafening as he displays a full mouth of straight teeth. He slams his fist lightly against the armrest twice.

Feeling hurt once more, I stare up at him. "Is that not true?"

Odin leans back, knocking his head against the throne, and stares up at the ceiling, still cackling. When he composes himself, he sits straight and glowers down at me. "Yes. It is true. But it is doubtful that this gift is going to be granted to you. It is a privilege only available to the winged Valkyries upon birth."

My head spins with disbelief. "But… but I have proven myself."

"That's what you say," Odin says with a booming voice. "But I see it as you breaking all the rules while on a vendetta to prove yourself and prove your worthlessness. It is not an act that I am going to honor."

A sleazy voice sounds from the front corner behind Odin. "I think that perhaps you should listen to the young, wingless Valkyrie." I stare in the direction of the voice, surprised to see the dark form of Loki stalking into the room. "Don't you think the young Valkyrie has worked hard to prove herself, blood brother?" Loki approaches the throne. His dark eyes never leave me.

"Don't be ridiculous, Loki," Odin snaps.

- CHAPTER TEN -

I stare at Loki with an open mouth. His dark eyes remain fixed on me until he reaches the throne.

"Don't you think that this Valkyrie has proven herself, my dear brother Odin? She has risked much for Asgard."

Odin swivels in his chair to look at Loki. "I don't know what you are thinking. But whatever it is, it isn't good. Put your evil plotting aside."

"Please listen to Loki, Odin." I try to gather some more flattery.

"There is a reason why I am called wise." Odin raises his chin. "It's because I won't listen to the likes of idiots like you. Guards!" The guards stand at attention. "Take that young wingless back to her academy and make sure you call Mistress Sigrun to punish her... academy style." He sneers down at me from over his large nose.

Knowing that no matter what I do, he isn't going to give me the right to reap souls for Valhalla, I call over my shoulder as I'm dragged out. "Loki, I need to speak with you." I hope that because Loki has stood up for me and asked for Odin to grant me this wish, he will speak to me. I am surprised that he came in and said his piece.

Loki says nothing, but his dark eyes don't leave me as I'm dragged unceremoniously out of the throne room. At least I'm not being locked up in the dungeons. I guess that is because Odin is keeping his promise to the dragons despite what he wants to do. Although he still won't treat the young dragons with the respect they deserve and use them as allies in fighting for Asgard and protecting against Ragnarök.

When Loki doesn't answer, I call out again. "Loki, please! I need to speak with you." The guards roughly drag me sideways, and I stumble over my feet. Somehow, I manage to stagger and stand upright, hoping that if I continue to peer over my shoulder, the god of mischief will speak with me.

Odin's expression does not waver, and Loki doesn't call me back, leaving me confused as I leave the throne room. I'm bombarded with disappointment. I was in the same room as Loki in his god form, and he still did not talk to me even though he stood up for me for a very brief moment. I don't understand. My mind spins. On top of all this information, he has now marked my friends.

Diligently, the guards march me past Birger and Gorm—the two guards stand at attention at the front door of the palace—and toward the academy as instructed by Odin. The thunderstorm that started prior to my visit to the palace continues as they march me through the land of Asgard and between the towering mountains. My slightly damp clothes become soaked, and the puddles splash up my legs, aided by the guards' footsteps as they march in unison.

The guard on the left shoves me harshly, and I turn to glare at him. There is no reason for this treatment. Suddenly, something blue dashes toward us. For a moment, my heart flutters with excitement. Maybe Naga is coming to intervene. But as I turn, all hope crashes at my feet. The figure is blue, yet it is the wrong shape. Charging from behind, on surprisingly quiet feet, is a frost giant. As I take him in, I am a little surprised. The frost giant that I fought with Elan's help was much larger. Looking at its smooth skin and smaller size, I think that perhaps this one is just a teenager. In any case, he's still huge in comparison to the three of us.

The guard on the left must have seen the shocked look on my face because he turns his head to peer over his shoulder before I have a chance to warn them. Instantly, he releases me, grabbing for his sword hanging by his side. The frost giant has a nasty scowl plastered on his face. His body is tense, and he seems ready to attack. I reach over my shoulder and grasp for my bow and arrow. My cheeks lose all feeling. I don't have my weapons with me. I suddenly feel naked. Since when don't I have my weapons on my back? I must have left them at Gilroma's. I go for my back pocket, reaching for my sling, only to grasp air. I must have been so preoccupied over my friends having magic that I committed the biggest sin of all—I forgot my weapons. The giant bounds forward in large, rapid steps, and both guards brace their swords with white knuckles, ready to defend. My mind spins, searching for another option to protect myself. Then it hits me, and I want to slam my palm against my forehead. My magic. How could I forget my magic?

Instantly, I gather the threads of magic coursing through my body. Except the giant is already upon us. One guard draws his sword back. He's ready to strike, but before he can drag it across his body, the giant slams his fist into the guard from the opposite direction. A massive grunt exits the guard as he projects through the air. He slams into the side of the mountain before sliding down its side and landing with a thud.

Without a moment's hesitation, the giant swings his other fist and flings the guard on my right into a large boulder not far away. A sickening crack reaches my ears, and my stomach churns with sickness, distracting me from gathering my magic. Before I know it, the giant is standing above me, and I stare up at him. My magic flees to the most unreachable part of my body.

Two large hands grasp me, pinning my arms by my sides, and he lifts me into the air. I wriggle and kick and bite the massive finger lying just under my mouth, but nothing makes the giant release his grip. My life is flashing before my eyes. This must be my end, and I haven't even managed to prove the wingless Valkyries' worth—or my own, for that matter—and I'm about to be crushed to death.

The giant spins to face the opposite direction and runs through the rain at a surprising speed for miles until eventually he reaches the Yggdrasil. Using one hand, he climbs down the branches of the world tree while still grasping me firmly in the other.

The End

Special Bonus – Deleted Scene

Go to https://dl.bookfunnel.com/2weanv19h7

to read a deleted scene from 'Warned' Valkyrie

Academy Dragon Alliance.

Abducted: Book 8 is released in December,

2019.

ACKNOWLEDGMENTS

I am touched by the enormous amount of support I have received from my immediate family. My husband has been a helpful first reader and at times been a wonderful motivator, with hints of ideas to help me through the blanks. The support from my three sons has also been overwhelming. They have put up with my head being in the clouds, thinking about the next plot twist or story for several years. Along with many hours spent working on my books and keeping in touch with my readers.

A big thank you to my extended family who support me being a book enthusiast.

A huge thank you to my editor, Neila F., her editing and writing tips, and my Proofreader, Libybet R. G., for picking up the things we missed.

Thank you to all of my readers who have loved my work, and continue to read my stories. I would love for you to share your thoughts in a review on one or all of the following:

Amazon.com
Goodreads
Barnes & Noble
You can follow Katrina Cope at:

https://www.facebook.com/Author.Katrina.Cope

https://twitter.com/Katrina_R_Cope

https://www.goodreads.com/author/show/7265107.Katrina_Cope

https://www.katrinacopebooks.com

http://http://www.amazon.com/Katrina-Cope/e/B00F00JF9M/

Book 8 of Valkyrie Academy Dragon Alliance Series 'Abducted' released December, 2019.

BOOKS BY KATRINA COPE

~~~~~

Pre-Teen Books

THE SANCTUM SERIES

JAYDEN'S CYBERMOUNTAIN

SCARLET'S ESCAPE

TAYLOR'S PLIGHT

ERIC & THE BLACK AXES

ADRIANNA'S SURGE

~~~~~

Young Adult Urban Fantasy

AFTERLIFE SERIES

FLEDGLING

THE TAKING

ANGELIC RETRIBUTION

DIVIDED PATHS

Afterlife Novelette

THE GATEKEEPER

~~~~~

Young Adult Urban Paranormal Fantasy

SUPERNATURAL EVOLVEMENT SERIES

(Associated with the Afterlife Series)

WITCH'S LEGACY (#0.5 Prequel)

AALIYAH

~~~~~

Young Adult Fantasy Nordic Myths

VALKYRIE ACADEMY DRAGON ALLIANCE SERIES

MARKED (Prequel)

CHOSEN

VANISHED

SCORNED

INFLICTED

EMPOWERED

AMBUSHED

WARNED

ABDUCTED

BESIEGED

GET UPDATES & NOTIFICATIONS OF GIVEAWAYS

Would you like a FREE copy of Marked?
Visit here:
https://www.katrinacopebooks.com/valkyrie-academy-dragon-alliance
Through this link you can sign up for my newsletter and receive a FREE copy of Marked plus updates about my fantasy books, sales and notification of giveaways.

DID YOU ENJOY THIS BOOK?
YOU CAN MAKE A BIG DIFFERENCE.

Honest reviews of my books help bring them to the attention of other readers.

If you've enjoyed this book, I'd be grateful if you could spend a few minutes leaving a review (it can be as short as you like).
The review can be left on Amazon and Goodreads.
Thank you very much.

ABOUT THE AUTHOR

Katrina is an author of several Young Adult and Preteen/Middle Grade novels. Each of her released books reaching the top 100 in certain categories on the Amazon's Best Sellers Rank – a few even as high as number one.

She resides in Queensland, Australia. Her three teenage boys and husband for over nineteen years treat her like a princess. Unfortunately though, this princess still has to do domestic chores.

From a very young age, she has been a very creative person and has spent many years travelling the world and observing many different personalities and cultures. Her favourite personalities have been the strange ones, yet the ones under the radar also hold a place in her heart.

During her last extensive travels, she spent 16 nights in a bomb shelter on a Kibbutz 8 kilometers off the Lebanese border. It was to avoid Katyusha bombs that the resident volunteers decided to name her after (she is still trying to work out why).

Katrina's online home is at
www.katrinacopebooks.com

You can connect with Katrina on:

Twitter https://twitter.com/Katrina_R_Cope

Facebook
https://www.facebook.com/Author.Katrina.Cope

Instagram
https://www.instagram.com/katrina_cope_author

Pinterest
https://www.pinterest.com.au/katrinacope56

Email authorkatrinacope@gmail.com

www.ingramcontent.com/pod-product-compliance
Lightning Source LLC
Chambersburg PA
CBHW022000130726
47903CB00014B/2639